Darcy
Swipes Left

For Chelsea Eberly, freditor extraordinaire ✮
& Liz Tardiff, who makes all things possible 🎨
—C.B.C.

Text copyright © 2016 by Penguin Random House LLC
Emoji copyright © Apple Inc.
Images on page 1, man © Shutterstock/Kiselev Andrey Valerevich,
house © Shutterstock/Shelli Jensen, sign © Shutterstock/Andy Dean Photography;
page 9 © Shutterstock/Masson; page 26 © Shutterstock/Creativa Images;
page 38 © Shutterstock/Nina Buday; pages 39 and 44 © Shutterstock/zentilia;
page 70 © Shutterstock/Mladen Mitrinovic; page 72 © Shutterstock/Iwona Wawro;
page 74 © Shutterstock/Matthew Dixon; page 85 © Shutterstock/YaroslavUrban;
page 87 © Shutterstock/jalcaraz; page 108 © Shutterstock/Marben

Library of Congress Cataloging-in-Publication Data is available upon request.
ISBN 978-1-101-94052-5 (trade) — ISBN 978-1-101-94053-2 (ebook)

MANUFACTURED IN CHINA
10 9 8 7 6 5 4 3 2 1
First Edition

Darcy
Swipes Left

jane austen

+

courtney carbone

Random House 🏠 New York

who's who

Mr. Bennet, master of Longbourn

Mrs. Bennet, lady of Longbourn

Jane Bennet, 1st daughter

Lizzy Bennet, 2nd daughter

Mary Bennet, 3rd daughter

Kitty Bennet, 4th daughter

Lydia Bennet, 5th daughter

Mr. Collins, the Bennets' distant relative

Mr. Gardiner, Lizzy's uncle

Mrs. Gardiner, Lizzy's aunt

Sir William Lucas, master of Lucas Lodge

Lady Lucas, lady of Lucas Lodge

Charlotte Lucas, Lizzy's BFF

Fitzwilliam Darcy, master of Pemberley

Send

🌸 Georgiana Darcy, Darcy's younger sister

👵 Lady Catherine de Bourgh, Darcy's aunt and lady of Rosings Estate

💂 Colonel Fitzwilliam, soldier and Darcy's cousin

💂 George Wickham, soldier and Darcy's ex-BFF

🔑 Mrs. Reynolds, Pemberley housekeeper

👨 Charles Bingley, master of Netherfield Park

👸 Caroline Bingley, Bingley's sister

👰 Louisa Hurst, Bingley's sister

👳 Mr. Hurst, Bingley's brother-in-law

💂 Colonel Forster

👩 Mrs. Forster

💂 Lieutenant Denny

💰 Mary King, Wickham's love interest

Mrs. Bennet

Top 5 Things Rich Men Want
[TeaFeed article]
1. A Wife

Click to read!

👍 REPLY

Lady Lucas: Duh, everyone knows that!

✅ Mr. Bingley has checked into Netherfield Park.

👍 Mrs. Bennet, Lady Lucas, and 20 others like this.

Mrs. Bennet

OMG, babe, guess who just bought Netherfield Park!

Charles Bingley 💰😊🎩🇬🇧

Send

> 👩 Mrs. Bennet
>
> **Mrs. Bennet took a quiz.**
> *Using one emoji, describe your daughters.*
> Jane: 😇
> Lizzy: 💡
> Mary: 📕
> Kitty: 😍
> Lydia: 😘
>
> 👍 Kitty likes this. REPLY

Mrs. Bennet

I'm so over Bingley!! He just moved in 🏠 & it's all anyone talks about anymore!! 😴

Mr. Bennet

If I knew you were 😷 of him, I wouldn't have gone over there this morning. 😉

Mrs. Bennet

WHAT? OMG! Best husband everrr!!! 💚

● ● ●

Send

Mrs. Bennet

Lady Lucas, what did your husband say about Mr. Bingley?!?! I need details!! 😉

Lady Lucas

Young! Handsome! Charming! #AllTheThings

And that he'll be GOING TO OUR BALL. 💃

Mrs. Bennet

OMG!!! We'll be there! 🏖️ 🍹

🎉 Dancer 🎉

Charles Bingley asks Charlotte Lucas to dance.

Charlotte Lucas accepts. #SwipesRight ✖ ♥

Charles Bingley asks Jane Bennet to dance.

Jane Bennet accepts. #SwipesRight ✖ ♥

Send

Charles Bingley asks
Jane Bennet to dance again.

 Jane Bennet accepts.
#SwipesRight

 Charles Bingley suggests
Fitzwilliam Darcy ask
Elizabeth Bennet to dance.

 Fitzwilliam Darcy declines.
#SwipesLeft

↳ Bingley: Darcy, c'mon! U
really not going to dance with
anyone?

Darcy: Your sisters are all taken.
None of these other girls are
good enough 4 me. 👎
You got the prettiest 1. 💁

Bingley: I know, right?
#SorryNotSorry

Bingley: But her sister Lizzy
seems cool.

Darcy: Meh. Not hot. Besides, if
no1 else wants her, why should I?

Bingley: You are the WORST
wingman. 😔

Send

Jane

Lizzy, dance w/ that hot guy Darcy! 😘 🔥

Lizzy

Look at your Dancer feed. He's a jerk. 😠

Jane

Maybe it was an accidental swipe left?! 😕

Lizzy

Whatevs. I won't let a guy like that ruin my night.

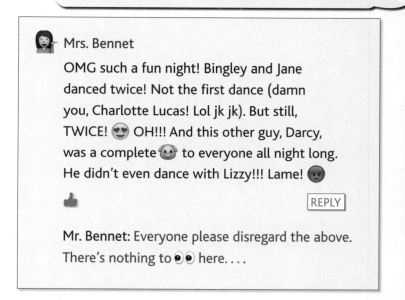

Mrs. Bennet

OMG such a fun night! Bingley and Jane danced twice! Not the first dance (damn you, Charlotte Lucas! Lol jk jk). But still, TWICE! 😍 OH!!! And this other guy, Darcy, was a complete 🐷 to everyone all night long. He didn't even dance with Lizzy!!! Lame! 😠

👍   REPLY

Mr. Bennet: Everyone please disregard the above. There's nothing to 👀 here. . . .

Send

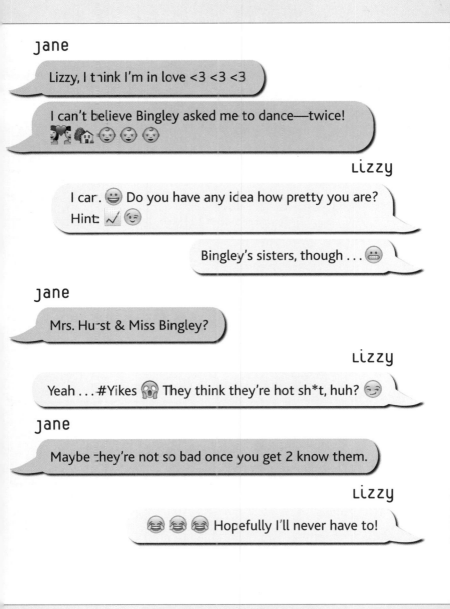

Group text: Jane, Charlotte, Lizzy

jane

Charlotte, Bingley danced with you first!

charlotte

But he danced with you twice! 🍀

Darcy really should have danced with Lizzy.

lizzy

He had me on his Not Hot list, that's for sure.
I needed an extra shawl for all that #Shade.

charlotte

SMH. Ya, he's stuck up. But let's be real . . . he has reason
2 b, with his 💰 and everything else going for him.

lizzy

I'd be cool with his pride if he didn't trample 🐘
on mine. #HatersGonnaHate

Send

📚 Mary Bennet

A person may be proud
without being vain.

👍   [REPLY]

Lizzy

IDK why u play it so cool w/ Bingley, Jane. ⛄
He's not going to know u 🖤 him!

Jane

That's the whole point! Wait & 👀. 😍

Send

Charlotte

Ladies, 9x out of 10, u should act more into a guy than u feel, to keep him interested. 😘 That's the best way to 🔒 it down. 💍 👰 💐 Happiness in 💏 is a matter of chance. 🎲

👍

REPLY

Lizzy: 😞 You don't rly mean that.

Charlotte: Yes & the less u know about a man before u 💒, the better! 🙈 🙉 🙊

Lizzy: Haha, or u could always play hard 2 get! 😏

BACK **DARCY** +

I may have been wrong about Lizzy. The more I 👀 her, the more I'm into her. 💚 I have 2 find out more.... Looking forward to the ball @ Sir Lucas's.

Send

🎉 **Dancer** 🎉

🎩 Sir William Lucas suggests Fitzwilliam Darcy ask Elizabeth Bennet to dance.

Fitzwilliam Darcy asks Elizabeth Bennet to dance.

Elizabeth Bennet declines. #SwipesLeft ⓧ ▾

MISS BINGLEY

What's up, Darcy? Wanna get out of here?

DARCY

I've just been thinking about how much I 🩵 a girl with a nice set.

MISS BINGLEY

EXCUSE ME ‼️⁉️

DARCY

Of 👀. lol

Send

jane

Mom, can I borrow the carriage?

Mrs. Bennet

No. Go on 🐎 so when it 🌧, they'll invite you to sleep over! zzᶻ

jane

R u serious? 😧

Mrs. Bennet

Completely.

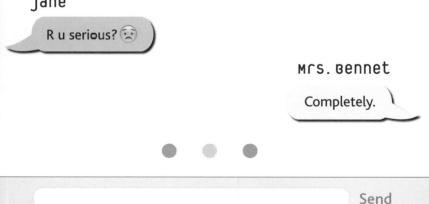

Send

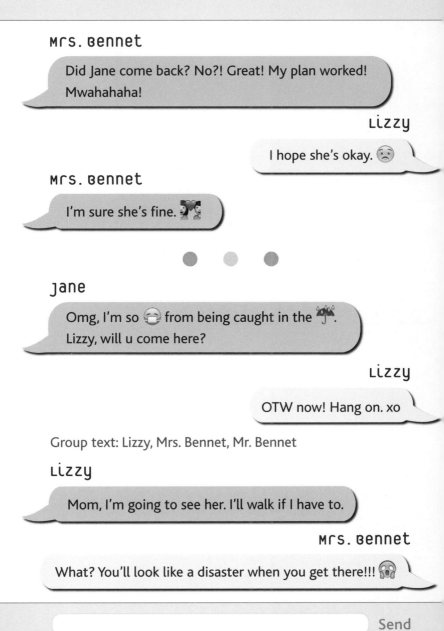

Mrs. Bennet

Did Jane come back? No?! Great! My plan worked! Mwahahaha!

Lizzy

I hope she's okay. 😟

Mrs. Bennet

I'm sure she's fine. 👭

● ● ●

Jane

Omg, I'm so 🤢 from being caught in the ☔. Lizzy, will u come here?

Lizzy

OTW now! Hang on. xo

Group text: Lizzy, Mrs. Bennet, Mr. Bennet

Lizzy

Mom, I'm going to see her. I'll walk if I have to.

Mrs. Bennet

What? You'll look like a disaster when you get there!!! 😱

Send

Lizzy

I don't care what I'll look like. All I care about is my sister! 👭

Mr. Bennet

Are you sure, Lizzy?

Lizzy

Yes, it's only a couple miles. 💪

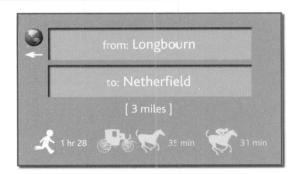

from: Longbourn

to: Netherfield

[3 miles]

🏃 1 hr 28   🛻 35 min   🏇 31 min

 Lizzy has checked into Netherfield.

👍 Jane likes this.

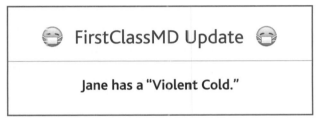

😷 FirstClassMD Update 😷

Jane has a "Violent Cold."

Send

Jane

... still sick ... glad i have Lizzy by my side.

👍 Lizzy likes this. | REPLY |

Bingley: Get better soon!
Miss Bingley: Ugh. Being sick is the worst. I hope that never happens 2 me! Gross!!!

Group text: Mrs. Hurst, Bingley, Darcy, Miss Bingley

Mrs. Hurst

Did u guys see Lizzy when she showed up this a.m.? Her 👗 had 6 inches of mud on it! Lolz.

Bingley

TBH, I thought she looked great. 😀

Miss Bingley

Oh, come on. Darcy, tell him he's insane. #HotMess

Darcy

Actually, just #Hot.

Miss Bingley

😒 Wutever.

Send

Mrs. Hurst

She's nice, but her 👪 is a disaster & they don't have any connections. So sad! 😢

Miss Bingley

They're sooooo poor, lolz. Thank goodness we're not poor! 😂

Group text: Lizzy, Miss Bingley, Bingley, Mrs. Hurst

Lizzy

Hey, Jane is 😴. Where r u guys?

Miss Bingley

Playing 🎴 s. We can deal u in.

Lizzy

No thx. I'm just gonna catch up on my reading. 📖

Miss Bingley

Lizzy hates everything except reading.

Lizzy

???

Send

18

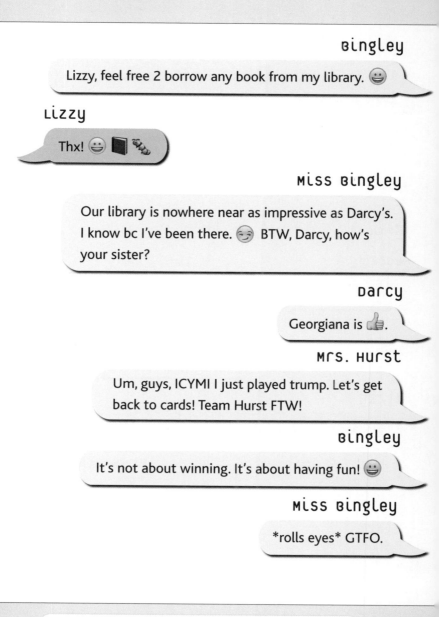

Miss Bingley
Wut do men 👀 4 in a woman? Wut does it mean 2 b accomplished?

👍 REPLY

Mrs. Hurst: They should b good @ crafting, DIY, etc. You know, the usual.
Darcy: If those are "the usual" skills every girl has, then why does that make them accomplished? Your standards r 2 low. 📈
Miss Bingley: She must also b good @ 🎵 💃 📝 🎨 🎹 🎿 ⛷️ 🏌️ 🎳 ....
Lizzy: 😂 Is that all?
Miss Bingley: She should have a certain something in the way she walks and talks . . . be expressive & well spoken. Etc.
Darcy: And she should always want 2 better herself with 📕.
Lizzy: Good luck finding her! 🍀

Send

✅ Mrs. Bennet, Kitty, and Lydia have checked into Netherfield.

 Mrs. Bennet
The gang's all here! Hooray! Oooh, nice drapes!

👍 REPLY

Group text: Mrs. Bennet, Miss Bingley, Lydia, Bingley

MRS. BENNET

I can't believe my poor Jane is still so 🤒!!! 😫 She's been here for days now. I do hope Bingley's taking good care of my beautiful, sweet, very single Jane!

MISS BINGLEY

We are giving her the best care possible. 🍵 💊

LYDIA

bingley, when r u gonna have a ball???? 🙏

BINGLEY

Oh, um, we'll figure it out when Jane is better. 😅

Send

Miss Bingley

Oh, Charles, u r so easy 2 sway. #PushOver

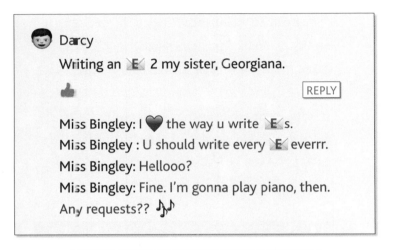

Darcy

Writing an 📧 2 my sister, Georgiana.

👍   REPLY

Miss Bingley: I 🖤 the way u write 📧s.
Miss Bingley : U should write every 📧 everrr.
Miss Bingley: Hellooo?
Miss Bingley: Fine. I'm gonna play piano, then.
Any requests?? 🎵

🎉 **Dancer** 🎉

Fitzwilliam Darcy asks
Elizabeth Bennet to dance.

Elizabeth Bennet declines.
#SwipesLeft ❎ 🤍

Send

BACK **LIZZY** +

Today was so weird. Miss Bingley showed off on the piano (so "accomplished"!), and Darcy asked me to dance again. Then I played the piano 🎵, and I'm 💯% sure I caught Darcy staring at me while i was playing. WTF is that guy's deal?? No worries, bc Jane is almost better, so I can go 🏠 soon!! 🙌

BACK **DARCY** +

Today was so awesome. Lizzy played piano 4 us & I totally stared @ her the whole time. She had no freaking clue. 😏 Man, I have 2 keep reminding myself that she is poor w/ no connections. FML. 😔

Send

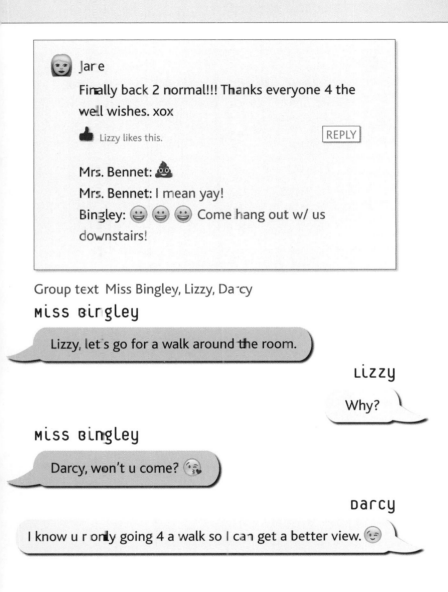

😊 Jane
Finally back 2 normal!!! Thanks everyone 4 the
well wishes. xox
👍 Lizzy likes this.   REPLY

Mrs. Bennet: 💩
Mrs. Bennet: I mean yay!
Bingley: 😀 😀 😀 Come hang out w/ us
downstairs!

Group text Miss Bingley, Lizzy, Darcy

Miss Bingley

Lizzy, let's go for a walk around the room.

Lizzy

Why?

Miss Bingley

Darcy, won't u come? 😘

Darcy

I know u r only going 4 a walk so I can get a better view. 😉

Send

Darcy

Darcy has taken a quiz:
What's your biggest weakness?

RESULT: Too Critical. Your good opinion, once lost, is gone forever. 👋

REPLY

Lizzy: Sweet weakness. I'll keep it in mind for job interviews.
Darcy: Don't hate. There's something wrong w/ everyone.
Lizzy: Me? Hate?? U r the one who chooses 2 hate everyone, my friend. #SeeAbove #SlowClap
Darcy: And u r the 1 who chooses 2 👀 the 😈 in me always.
Lizzy: Touché.

Send

Lizzy leaves Netherfield tomorrow. Not sure how I feel about that. I hate 2 admit it, but she s kinda growing on me. ✓ Plus, it's hysterical 2 c Bingley's sister freak out. She's insanely jealous. (Or maybe just insane?) 😂

✅ Jane and Lizzy have checked into Longbourn.

👍 Mr Bennet and Miss Bingley like this.

Jane: Home at last!
Bingley: Hope u got there safely. 😄

Send

To: **The Bennet Family**

From: Mr. William Collins

When: Monday, November 18, at 4pm

What: I'm coming over so I can apologize 4 inheriting ur estate as the closest male relative. Sucks that u'll be homeless if Mr. Bennet dies. 😵 Can't wait 2 👀 the 🏠! Ur welcome!

cc: Lady Catherine de Bourgh

 Mrs. Bennet

😫 I HATE that a random relative that we don't even KNOW is inheriting our estate, just bc we don't have any sons. 👬 BUT maybe he'll want 2 💍 1 of our daughters. 👭 🙏

👍   REPLY

Lydia: is he a soldier?

Mrs. Bennet: Nope! He's a clergyman.

Lydia: *swipes left*

Send

Mr. Collins

Dinner at my future house! #NomNomNom

👍 [REPLY]

Collins: Lady Catherine de Bourgh, wish you were here!
Lady Catherine de Bourgh: I'm most certainly glad I'm not. —LCdB
Lydia: i wish those soldiers we saw today were here! 💂🖤💂🖤
Kitty: *fans herself*
Lizzy: SMH
Lady Catherine de Bourgh: I do not approve of acronyms, improper punctuation, or the silly little pictures you are employing. How do I report? —LCdB

collins

Mrs. Bennet, I think it's only right 4 me 2 offer marriage 2 one of ur daughters, so that the 🏠 stays in the 👨‍👩‍👧 once I inherit it. Therefore, I've decided I would be willing to marry Jane. 💍 #HumbleBrag

Send

Mrs. Bennet

😁 OoOoOoh, well, that's a very good idea, though Jane is prob going 2 marry someone else very soon. (Bingley) *wink wink*

collins

Ah. I see. Well then, how about the next prettiest?

Mrs. Bennet

Lizzy? 💍 ?

collins

Perfect! I'll start looking at venues.

Send

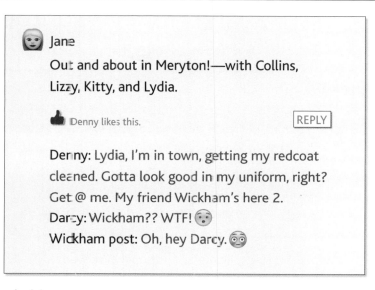

Jane

Out and about in Meryton!—with Collins, Lizzy, Kitty, and Lydia.

👍 Denny likes this. REPLY

Denny: Lydia, I'm in town, getting my redcoat cleaned. Gotta look good in my uniform, right? Get @ me. My friend Wickham's here 2.
Darcy: Wickham?? WTF! 😯
Wickham post: Oh, hey Darcy. 😳

wickham

Nice meeting you @ your aunt's party, Lizzy. Not to change the subject, but do u know how long Darcy will be in town? #TBT #Awkward

Lizzy

IDK, how do u know him?

wickham

Long 📖 short, we've known each other since we were 😊 😊, when my father was his father's steward. 💼

Send

Lizzy

Is it just me, or does that guy suck? 👎

wickham

😃 I'm biased, but yeah. Glad you agree! We used to be BFFs. Darcy's father 🖤ed me. He promised to help me pay for my dream job in the ⛪! I would have made an awesome pastor. 🙏 🙌 But when he died, Darcy plotted against me and made sure I didn't get it. 😠

Same w/ his sister, Georgiana. I thought we were #Meant2B, but now we don't even talk. 😶

Lizzy

😔!

wickham

Yep, but maybe keep it between us. 🙊

Lizzy

I feel bad 4 whatever girl ends up w/ him!

Send

wickham

Yeah, he's supposed to Lady Catherine de Bourgh's daughter.

Lizzy

Oh? I hear she's 😔. That poor girl can't catch a break. #SoSad

wickham

Yeah . . . but my story is sadder, right??

● ○ ●

Lizzy

I HAVE to tell you what Wickham told me last night. ⚠️

Lizzy

Hold on. I'll send you the messages. . . .

Jane

OMG, is this true? Could Darcy really have done all those terrible things to Wickham? 😈 I can't believe it. 🙅 Bingley thinks so highly of him. 😇

Lizzy

Why would Wickham make it up? It's DARCY we're talking about. Even *you* can't deny what a jerk he is!

Jane

Darcy can't be all bad. Maybe it's a misunderstanding?

Lizzy

<Sigh> You're 2 nice, Jane.

🧑 **Bingley**

Bingley has created an event:
Ball at Netherfield.

👍 Mrs. Bennet, Kitty, and Lydia like this. | REPLY |

Wickham: Out of town on business—sorry!

👍 Darcy likes this.

Send

🎉 Dancer 🎉

Elizabeth Bennet's 1st Dance is now available.

Mr. Collins asks Elizabeth Bennet to dance.

Elizabeth Bennet reluctantly accepts. #SwipesRight

Elizabeth Bennet's 2nd Dance is now available.

Mr. Collins asks Elizabeth Bennet to dance.

Elizabeth Bennet very reluctantly accepts. #SwipesRight

Fitzwilliam Darcy askes Elizabeth Bennet to dance.

Elizabeth Bennet accepts to avoid Mr. Collins. #SwipesRight

↪ Mr. Collins: NOOOOOOOOOO

Send

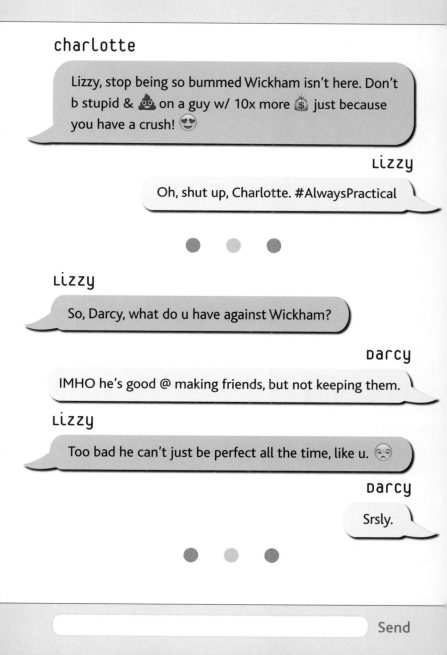

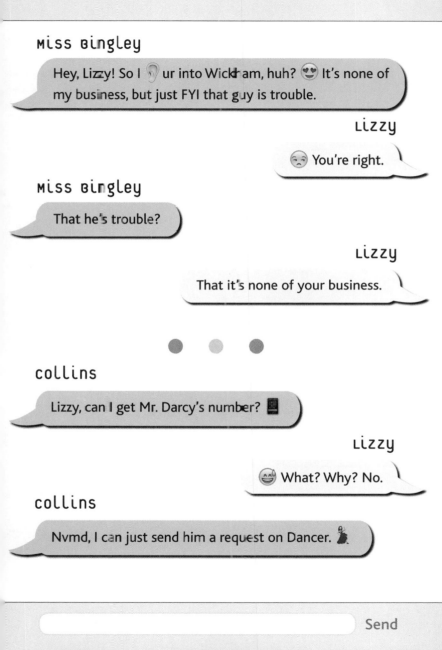

Lizzy

Absolutely do not do that. 🚫 So uncool!!!! 👎😱😬

collins

Too late! ⏱️

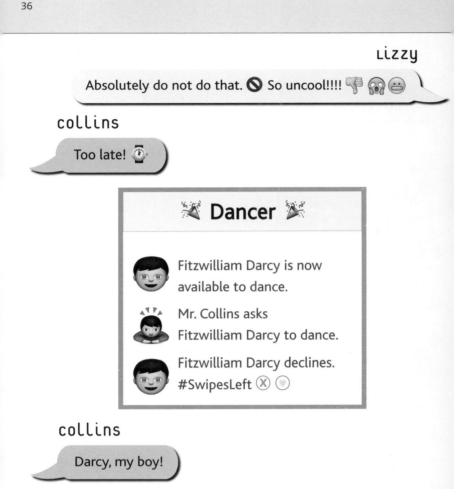

🎉 **Dancer** 🎉

Fitzwilliam Darcy is now available to dance.

Mr. Collins asks Fitzwilliam Darcy to dance.

Fitzwilliam Darcy declines. #SwipesLeft ❌ 🤍

collins

Darcy, my boy!

Darcy

Do I know you? 😠

Send

collins

I'll give u a hint. Check out our mutual friends. 😏

Mr. Collins and Darcy have one friend in common:
👩 Lady Catherine de Bourgh

Pretty cool, huh?

Darcy?

Darcy?

🚫 Darcy has added Collins to Blocked Callers List.

Send

Mrs. Bennet

Mrs. Bennet has created a wedding board:

Jane Bennet and Charles Bingley

👍 REPLY

Jane: Mom, take that down!!!! Everyone can 👀.
Lizzy: Srsly, delete this!
Mrs. Bennet: Why?? Lizzy, Jane marrying 💰
means u might marry 💰 2! #Blessed

Send

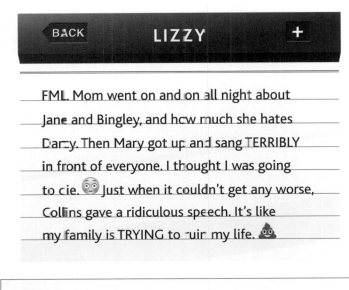

BACK **LIZZY** +

FML. Mom went on and on all night about Jane and Bingley, and how much she hates Darcy. Then Mary got up and sang TERRIBLY in front of everyone. I thought I was going to die. 😳 Just when it couldn't get any worse, Collins gave a ridiculous speech. It's like my family is TRYING to ruin my life. 💩

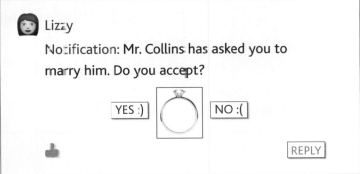

Lizzy

Notification: Mr. Collins has asked you to marry him. Do you accept?

YES :) | NO :(

REPLY

Lizzy

WTF?! Collins, why do you want to get married?!

Send

collins

I knew u would ask, so I made this 📝.

Reasons 2 Get Married
#1 Lady Catherine de Bourgh wants me to. ☆
#2 Happiness 😄 🌈 ☀
#3 To set a good example for my parish ⛪
#4 FOMO
#5 YOLO

Lizzy

No, I mean . . . why do you want to get married to ME?

collins

Lots of ladies want 2 marry me, but since I'm inheriting ur father's estate, I should marry 1 of his daughters to make every1 😄. I'm such a nice guy, I won't even make him give me a dowry! 💰 💰 💰

Lizzy

Hold up. ✋ I'm not marrying u. Thx, but no.

collins

Aw, r u doin that thing where u say no but u rly mean yes? So cute.

Send

Lizzy

No means no.

collins

But I have 💵! And connections (LCdB)! And no one else may ever ask you! Your biological 🕐 is ticking, u know. . . .

Lizzy

😒 Don t make this harder than it has to be. It's not happening. 🙅

collins

Adorable. I will take it up w/ ur parents, then.

Group text: Mrs. Bennet, Mr. Bennet, Lizzy

Mrs. Bennet

Lizzy, if you don't marry Mr. Collins I will never 👀 you again!!! 😡

Mr. Bennet

Well, you have a difficult decision to make, Lizzy. Because if you DO marry Mr. Collins, I'LL never 👀 u again. 😇

Send

Lizzy

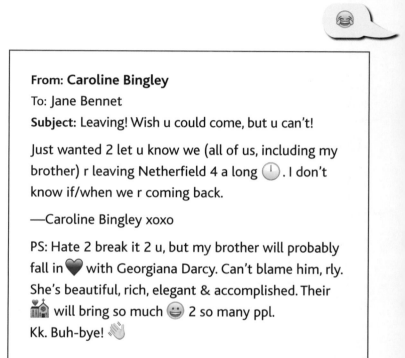

From: **Caroline Bingley**
To: Jane Bennet
Subject: Leaving! Wish u could come, but u can't!

Just wanted 2 let u know we (all of us, including my brother) r leaving Netherfield 4 a long 🕐. I don't know if/when we r coming back.

—Caroline Bingley xoxo

PS: Hate 2 break it 2 u, but my brother will probably fall in 🖤 with Georgiana Darcy. Can't blame him, rly. She's beautiful, rich, elegant & accomplished. Their 💒 will bring so much 😀 2 so many ppl.
Kk. Buh-bye! 👋

jane

Lizzy, I just got the worst 📰 ! 😭

Bingley is leaving and never coming back! 😭

Send

Lizzy

WHAT?! Jane, this doesn't sound like something he would do. I bet his sisters are behind it. 😠

Jane

Maybe, but what difference does it make now? 💔

BACK **MR. COLLINS** **+**

List of People 2 Marry:

~~Jane~~

~~Lizzy~~

Charlotte

Mary

Lydia

Kitty

Send

44

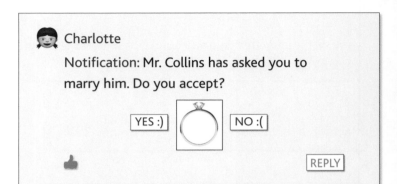

Charlotte

Notification: Mr. Collins has asked you to marry him. Do you accept?

YES :)   NO :(

REPLY

BACK   **CHARLOTTE**   +

Should I Marry Mr. Collins??

Pros
Comfortable 🏠
Connections ☎
Good character 🎩
Situation in life 🏛💰
Don't have to become a governess 👩👶

Cons
Being married to Mr. Collins 😣

Send

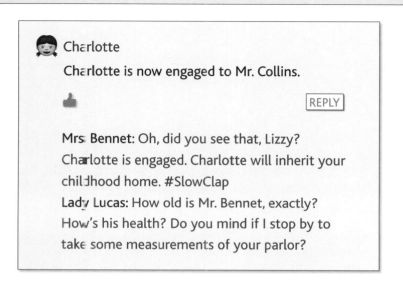

Charlotte

Charlotte is now engaged to Mr. Collins.

REPLY

Mrs. Bennet: Oh, did you see that, Lizzy? Charlotte is engaged. Charlotte will inherit your childhood home. #SlowClap

Lady Lucas: How old is Mr. Bennet, exactly? How's his health? Do you mind if I stop by to take some measurements of your parlor?

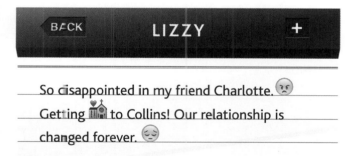

BACK   LIZZY   +

So disappointed in my friend Charlotte. 😠 Getting 💒 to Collins! Our relationship is changed forever. 😔

Send

- Volume 2 -

From: Caroline Bingley
To: Jane Bennet
Subject: London is the BEST

Greetings from London! Bingley is sry he didn't get 2 say a proper good-bye when we left Netherfield (probably 4ever).
Luv ya!
—Caroline Bingley xx
PS: Georgiana Darcy is even prettier IRL than I remembered! 🖤

Jane

Bingley's never coming back. 😫

Lizzy

I'm so sorry, Jane.

Ur an 🎩. I 🖤 u. The more I 👀 of the 🌍, the less I understand it.

Send

Lizzy

1) How could Bingley leave you?

2) How could Charlotte marry Collins? WTF?

Jane

Oh, Lizzy. Don't be so harsh!

Lizzy

I'm not being harsh. I'm being honest!

Mrs. Gardiner

Surprise, Lizzy! Your uncle and I are coming to visit. It's a Christmas miracle! 🎅 🎁 🎄

Lizzy

You're in town?! Hooray! What a good 🎁! 😀 😀 😀

Mrs. Gardiner

Yes, and I want to hear ALL your thoughts on Bingley and Jane. Do you think he was really into her? 😍

Send

Lizzy

Definitely! He ignored everyone else and only paid attention to her. When he left, it was so weird.

Mrs. Gardiner

😔 Do you think Jane would come back to London with us?

Lizzy

Good idea! I bet she would. 👍👍

Mrs. Gardiner

Excellent! And I want YOU to come with us on vacation later this year!

Lizzy

Count me in! Thx, Auntie! 😎

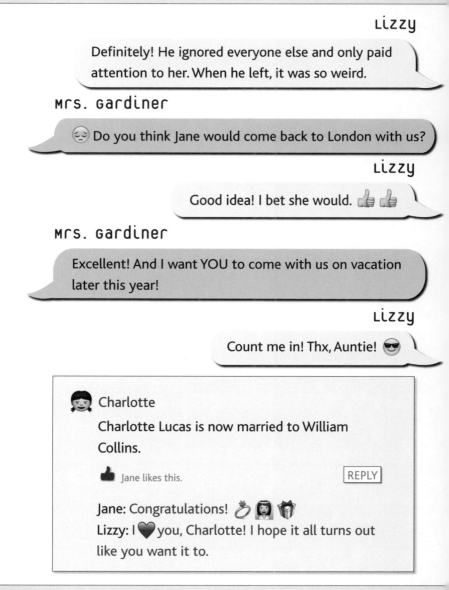

Charlotte

Charlotte Lucas is now married to William Collins.

👍 Jane likes this.

REPLY

Jane: Congratulations! 💍👰🎁
Lizzy: I 🖤 you, Charlotte! I hope it all turns out like you want it to.

Send

From: Jane Bennet
To: Lizzy Bennet
Subject: Lonely in London

Lizzy!

It's been 4 weeks and I still haven't run into Bingley. 🤢 His sister waited 2 weeks(!) to say hi. 😔 When she did come over, she was so incredibly rude. I don't want 2 b friends 👭 w/ her anymore. Maybe she's protective of Bingley?? But that doesn't make sense oc he's completely ghosted me anyway. 👻 No 📱 no ✉️, no 💌. Nothing. 😔 💔 Caroline even said he knew I was here. Maybe I'll never find 🖤. Time to start collecting 🐱s! Hope things are better on your end.
xox Jane

💰 Miss King

Miss King has inherited a lot of 💰.

👍 Wickham likes this.

REPLY

Send

Mrs. Gardiner

Lizzy, don't you think it's odd that Wickham hooked up with Miss King so quickly after she came into money?

Lizzy

I don't think he's a gold digger, if that's what you're getting @.

Mrs. Gardiner

You said it—not me!

 Lizzy has checked into Hunsford Parsonage.

👍 Charlotte likes this.

Charlotte: Thanks for visiting! The next 6 weeks are going to be awesome!!
Collins: Can't wait to show u what u've been missing, Lizzy. 😉

Send

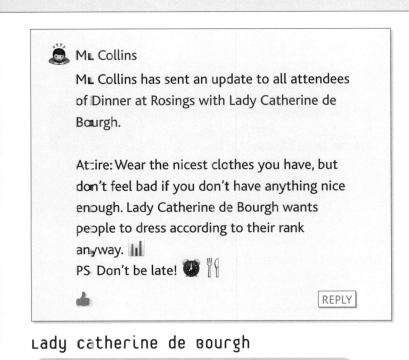

Mr Collins

Mr Collins has sent an update to all attendees of Dinner at Rosings with Lady Catherine de Bourgh.

Attire: Wear the nicest clothes you have, but don't feel bad if you don't have anything nice enough. Lady Catherine de Bourgh wants people to dress according to their rank anyway.
PS Don't be late!

👍 | REPLY

Lady catherine de bourgh

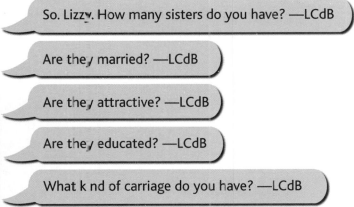

So. Lizzy. How many sisters do you have? —LCdB

Are they married? —LCdB

Are they attractive? —LCdB

Are they educated? —LCdB

What kind of carriage do you have? —LCdB

Send

LIZZY

Oh wow. Where to begin? So many questions! 😃

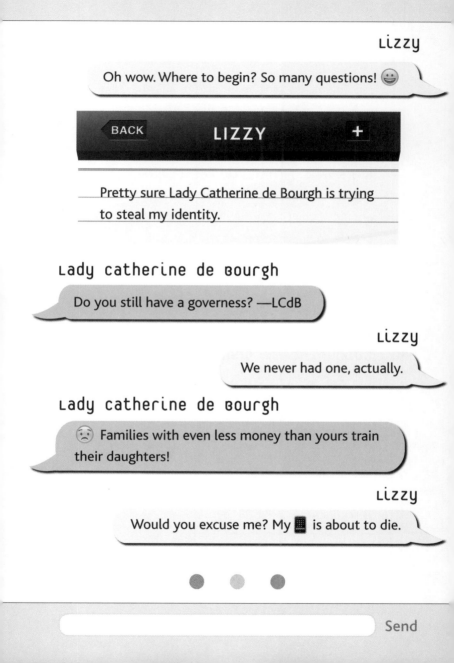

| ◀ BACK | **LIZZY** | + |

Pretty sure Lady Catherine de Bourgh is trying to steal my identity.

Lady Catherine de Bourgh

Do you still have a governess? —LCdB

LIZZY

We never had one, actually.

Lady Catherine de Bourgh

😟 Families with even less money than yours train their daughters!

LIZZY

Would you excuse me? My 🔋 is about to die.

● ● ●

Send

collins

What did you think? Isn't Lady Catherine de Bourgh the best EVER? You're 🍀 she talked to you, Lizzy. You're so beneath her, you know. 😃

← BACK LIZZY +

I've been here for 2 weeks. We have gone to Rosings a # of times, all of which were terrible! 😖 But I did get some interesting —Darcy is coming tonight. I don't really want to see him, but it will be good for LCdB to have some fresh meat, not to mention I'll get to see how he acts with his "soul mate," Miss de Bourgh. #OTP 💜 Ha!

✅ Darcy and Colonel Fitzwilliam have checked into Rosings.

Send

Group text: Colonel Fitzwilliam, Lizzy, Darcy

Fitzwilliam

Lizzy, ditch LCdB and play piano for Darcy and me. 🎵

Lizzy

Fine, as long as Darcy doesn't scowl the whole time! 😠

Fitzwilliam

#TypicalDarcy lolz

Darcy

You and your snarky sense of humor, Lizzy.

Lizzy

Fitzwilliam, don't believe a word he says. Or I will start telling stories of my own. #MerytonBall

Darcy

I'm not afraid. Bring it on. 💪

Fitzwilliam

Well, now you have to tell me everything.

Send

Lizzy

I met Darcy at a ball. There were more girls than guys, but he refused to dance w/ anyone. 😣 And there were so many girls without partners! 🙍 #ChivalryIsDead

Darcy

In my defense, I didn't know anyone there. . . .

Lizzy

And that's the way you wanted it to stay!

How long can I keep texting without LCdB noticing? 😜 Fitzwilliam, are u timing this? ⌚

Darcy

Wait, what would you have had me do? Start going up to random people and introducing myself?

Lizzy

YES! It's ridiculous that with all your "class" and "sophistication" you can't so much as make small talk at a party. 🍰!

Send

Fitzwilliam

He obviously just didn't want to.

Darcy

Sry I'm not the best conversationalist.

Lizzy

Just bc you're not the best @ something doesn't mean u avoid it completely. Sometimes you just have to practice the things that intimidate u.

Darcy

Darcy

Hey, Lizzy, u home? I'm nearby.

Lizzy

I'm out walking.

Send

Darcy

This is a very nice 🏡. Collins is 🍀 to have ⛪ Charlotte, huh?

Lizzy

Srsly. He's very 🍀 to have met Charlotte, who was willing to look at the pros instead of the cons. 📊

Darcy

True. Okay, I g2g.

Lizzy

Ttyl.

☑ Charlotte has checked into Hunsford Parsonage.

charlotte

Darcy was here? What, is he like in 💜 with you now?

Lizzy

If he is, he has a strange way of showing it.

Send

Okay, so this is weird. Darcy showed up the other day in the park 🌿🌳🍃 I always walk in. 😔 He knows it's my fave place to go, right? But then the NEXT day he showed up AGAIN. 😟😟 He must have known he'd 🏃 into me. So why?? But—wait for it—the 3rd day the same thing happens, and he didn't even PRETEND it was an accident. 😟😟😟 He 🧍 right next to me and started chatting me up. 👫 Like, actual ❓s instead of just small talk. Maybe he wants to set me up w/ Fitz? WTF! I don't get that guy at all.‼️❓

Send

Lizzy

Hey, Fitz, r u guys heading out soon?

Fitzwilliam

We prob should, though Darcy keeps extending our trip.

Lizzy

Really?! Well, he's 🍀 to have you along for company.

Fitzwilliam

He's a good friend. 👬 And not just to me. I heard a 📖 the other day that he kept his friend from 💍 this girl who would have been a terrible match. 👸 I think it was his buddy Blingley? Bringley? Something like that.

Lizzy

Bingley. 😒 Tell me more . . . ?

Fitzwilliam

Well, I shouldn't say anything bc it would b bad if the girl's 👪 found out! 🙊

Lizzy

My 👄 are sealed. . . .

Send

Fitzwilliam

Apparently Bingley was going to 💍 into this crazy 👫. Think 😈-in-law! Haha! And Darcy wasn't even sure the girl liked his friend back. ⛄

Lizzy

WHAT?! 😡

Fitzwilliam

u OK?

Lizzy

Yeah, just . . . WTF. I don't get y Darcy would get involved. Esp. if his friend & the girl really were in 💑.

Like, deeply in 🖤!

Fitzwilliam

???

Lizzy

But, uh, who knows. Hard 2 say when u don't know all the details. 😅

Send

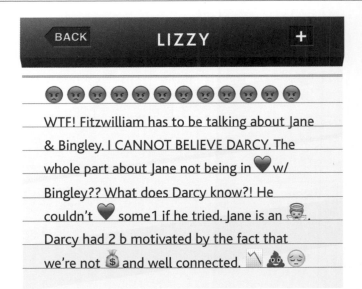

charlotte

Hey, Lizzy, we're about to leave 4 Rosings. R u ready?

Lizzy

I'm 😵. Going 2 lie down. ᴢᶻᶻ

charlotte

Okay, feel better! I'll check on you later. xo

Send

✅ Darcy has checked into Hunsford Parsonage.

Darcy

How are you? I heard you were 😷. Don't worry, you can stay in your room. But what I have to text cannot wait! ⏳ 💣 😄

Lizzy

Okay . . . ?

Darcy

Look. I've fought this for a long time. 💪 🕐 But I can't fight it anymore! I MUST tell you how ardently I 😍 you.

I mean, I know I could do a lot better. It's against my will, against my reason, and against my character. But I 🖤 who I 🖤. #FirstWorldProblems

Lizzy

😦

You know this is Lizzy, right?

Send

Darcy

Yes. And u have 2 marry me. 💍 Sure, your 👨‍👩‍👧 isn't as fancy as mine, but we'll work thru it.

Lizzy

Um, I guess I should b flattered, but 👎. I never wanted u 2 fall in 🖤 w/ me, and u obvi never wanted 2 either!! 😠 I hate hurting ur feelings, but u'll get over it.

Darcy

That's all u r going 2 say? You're not even going 2 tell me why?? 😖

Lizzy

You just said u like me against ur will, against ur better judgment & against ur character. WTF?! Even if I could 👀 past all that, I just found out from Fitz that u were the 1 who convinced Bingley to break up w/ my sister! 💔 Even if I did have feelings 4 u (which I don't!), do u rly think I would accept knowing what u did 2 Jane?

ADMIT IT!

Send

Darcy

I don't deny it. I did everything in my power 2 💔 them up. And I'm 😁 I did!

Lizzy

Ugh! And even before that happened, I hated u bc of what u did to Wickham.

Darcy

OMG what does Wickham have 2 do w/ anything??

Lizzy

You destroyed his life. #TypicalDarcy

Darcy

THIS is what u think of me? That I'm a 👿? Wow. I was just being honest, Lizzy. #SorryNotSorry

I call it how I 👀 it. Would you rather I flatter u w/ some bull 💩 compliments? Be all 🪰 and 🙈? What should I say? Congrats on having a ridiculous 👨‍👩‍👧! Congrats on having no connections! Congrats on being middle class! 🌂🌂🌂

Send

Lizzy

The *way* u asked me 2 💍 u doesn't even matter. It would have been a NO either way. You've been a conceited jerk since day 1. You're the last guy in the 🌍 I would marry. ⛪ 🙅

Darcy

I get it. And now I am 😳. Sry for taking up so much of your ⏰. Peace.

From: Fitzwilliam Darcy
To: Lizzy Bennet
Subject: Closure

Don't worry. I'm not going 2 try 2 convince u 2 ⛪ me. Pls just read this (even though u r 😠) because I need 2 clear stuff ⬆️.
Last night, u accused me of 2 things:
1) Breaking up Bingley & Jane 💔
2) Ruining Wickham's life 😭
Here goes:
Bingley was obvi in 🖤 w/ Jane. But I thought she just wasn't into him. Though I guess u would know better than me. My bad.

Send

But aside from Jane's 🖤 (or lack thereof), there is also the fact that your mother is 🤦‍♀️🤦‍♀️🤦‍♀️. And don't get me started on Lydia, Kitty, and Mary. 🙍‍♀️🙍‍♀️👀 Even ur father . . . Look, I'm not trying to hurt ur feelings. I'm just telling it like it is. 🙊

The only thing I feel bad about is that Bingley's sisters & I made sure he never found out Jane was in town. . . .

Now, Wickham. My dad thought Wickham was going 2 become a priest ⛪, but Wickham wanted 2 study law. 💼 When my dad died, Wickham and I agreed on a yearly allowance—a generous one. 💰 But instead of going 2 law school 🏫, he wasted it all. 💸 👯 🍺 🍹 🎲 He even had the nerve to come back & ask 4 more 💰💰! #Dirtbag

AND THAT'S WHEN HE WENT AFTER MY SISTER. 😡 She was living in London w/ a chaperone. The chaperone knew Wickham & together they cooked up 🔍 a plan 2 get our family's 💰. Wickham pretended 2 b in 😍 w/ Georgiana and convinced her to ELOPE. 👰 🐎 SMH. She told me just in 🕐. I confronted Wickham, and he 🏃.

I would have told u last night, but I didn't know where 2 start. I hope u understand. Everything I did

Send

was for the ppl I . Bingley, my sister, etc. If u don't believe me, u can ask my cousin Fitz.

Best,
Darcy

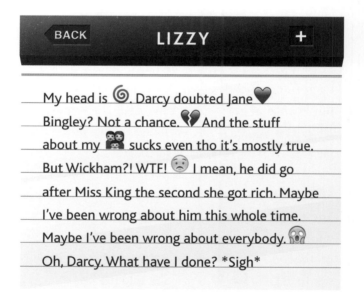

BACK   LIZZY   +

My head is 🌀. Darcy doubted Jane 🖤
Bingley? Not a chance. 💔 And the stuff
about my 👨‍👩‍👧 sucks even tho it's mostly true.
But Wickham?! WTF! 😞 I mean, he did go
after Miss King the second she got rich. Maybe
I've been wrong about him this whole time.
Maybe I've been wrong about everybody. 😱
Oh, Darcy. What have I done? *Sigh*

✅ Darcy and Fitzwilliam have checked out of Rosings.

Send

Group text: Lizzy, Mr. Collins, Charlotte

Lizzy

Time for me to head out. 🖐 Thanks for having me!

collins

Want me 2 give u Lady Catherine de Bourgh's contact info? So u can send her a thank u card 4 talking 2 u even though she's better than u?

Lizzy

Um, you can just say TY 4 me. Bye-bye!

charlotte

Safe travels, Lizzy. xo

● ● ●

Lizzy

Jane, I'm OTW 🏠 now. Darcy proposed 2 me. 💍 💐

jane

SERIOUSLY? Hurry to London! We have to talk asap!!

Send

✅ Lizzy has checked into London.

👍 Jane likes this.

🎩 **Wickham**

Wickham has changed his relationship status to single. 💔

👍 Lydia likes this.

REPLY

👧 **Lydia**

so 😭! all my 💂 💂 💂 r going 2 brighton. guess i'll go meet up w/ my much older sisters & bring them home!

👍 Mrs. Bennet likes this.

REPLY

📚 **Mary Bennet**

Who needs friends when you have books?

👍

REPLY

Send

Lizzy

Did u see the 📧 I fwded u from Darcy?

Jane

Can't believe it! 😨

Lizzy

Are you disappointed in me 4 saying no to him? 😔

Jane

Of course not!

Lizzy

What about all the stuff re: Wickham? It's crazy bc he seems like an 😇 and Darcy seems like a 😈, but it's actually the reverse! 🔄

Do u think we should tell every1? 📣

Jane

No. 🙅

Maybe Wickham's trying to be better? 😀

Send

Lizzy

Oh, Jane, that's cute. Let's hope so! 🙏

To: Lydia Bennet
From: Mrs. Forster

You're invited!

What: To stay with us in Brighton
When: This summer
Who: Me & my new hubby, Col. Forster . . .
and every hot 💂 **everrr.**

Lizzy

Dad, I REALLY don't think u should let Lydia go 2 Brighton. She ruins our 👨‍👩‍👧's rep. 📉 If u don't put her in ✔️ now, she'll be that way her whole life: a vapid, uncontrollable 😘 . Same with Kitty. 👩👩

Send

Mr. Bennet

Don't worry. No one will judge you based on your ridiculous 👨‍👩. Colonel Forster will keep her out of trouble. We don't have enough 💰 for someone to rip her off. The 🎩s will pass her over, and it will be a teachable moment. 🍎

Lizzy

I have a bad feeling about this.

Mr. Bennet

What could POSSIBLY go wrong?

✅ Wickham has checked into Longbourn.

Wickham

Hey, Lizzy! What's up? 😄

Lizzy

Just got back from Rosings. Spent 3 weeks with Darcy and his cousin Fitz. The convo was very revealing. 👿

Wickham

Ah, Fitz is v. different than his jerky cousin, amiright? 😉

Send

Lizzy

I've changed my mind re: Darcy.

I've changed my mind re: some other ppl 2. 😠

wickham

Is that so? ☹ Um, g2g.

👧 Lydia Bennet

Lydia and Kitty have posted 120 photos to the album: Selfies w/ Soldiers.

👍 Mrs. Bennet likes this.   REPLY

Mr. Bennet: 👎 You two are the silliest girls in 🇬🇧!

👧 Lizzy

Lizzy has posted an album: Touring the Lakes w/ Uncle and Aunt Gardiner.

👍   REPLY

Send

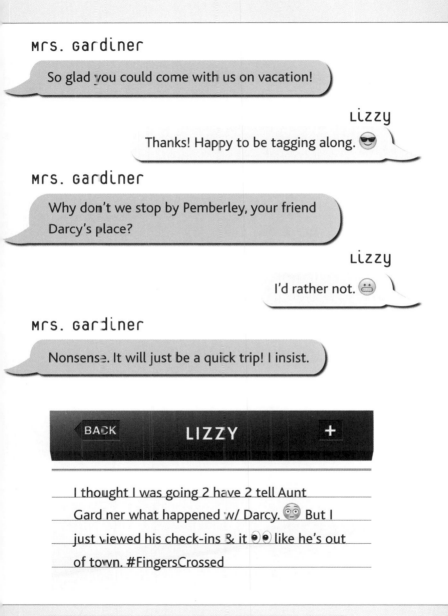

Mrs. Gardiner

So glad you could come with us on vacation!

Lizzy

Thanks! Happy to be tagging along. 😎

Mrs. Gardiner

Why don't we stop by Pemberley, your friend Darcy's place?

Lizzy

I'd rather not. 😬

Mrs. Gardiner

Nonsense. It will just be a quick trip! I insist.

BACK   **LIZZY**   +

I thought I was going 2 have 2 tell Aunt Gardner what happened w/ Darcy. 😳 But I just viewed his check-ins & it 👀 like he's out of town. #FingersCrossed

Send

- Volume 3 -

 Mrs. Gardiner, Mr. Gardiner, and Lizzy have checked into Pemberley.

👍 Mrs. Reynolds likes this.

Mrs. Reynolds: Welcome! Giving tours of the estate is my favorite thing about being the 🏡 keeper. 🗝️

Lizzy: Wow. I've never 👀 anywhere more beautiful in the whole 🌍. Whoever 👰 Darcy will be a very 🍀 woman!

✅ Darcy has checked into Pemberley.

Mrs. Gardiner: Lizzy——look! Your friend Darcy is here, too.

Darcy: Lizzy, ur here??

Lizzy: Hiii 😳

Darcy: What r u doing here?

Lizzy: Just passing thru. My aunt & uncle wanted 2 stop by.

Darcy: When did u leave Longbourn?

Lizzy: Recently.

Darcy: Gotcha. Well, I have 2 🏃. But I'll brb!

Send

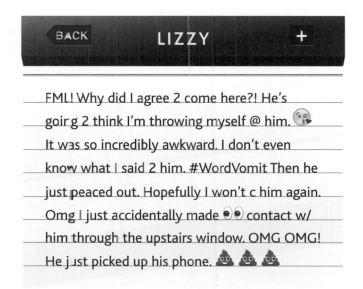

Darcy

Peeping is a crime, u know. 😉

Lizzy

FYI I didn't think u were going 2 b here. Mrs. Reynolds said u weren't coming back till tomorrow.

Darcy

Had 2 come back early. Bingley & his sisters r coming tomorrow. My sister will be coming 2. She wants to meet u & I want u to meet her. 😃

Send

Lizzy

😧 Cool, yeah.

Darcy

Do you want to come inside for a drink? 🍹

Lizzy

I think we r heading out now. But I'll see u tomorrow.

Darcy

Sounds good!

BACK   **LIZZY**   +

😃 😄 😃

● ● ●

Bingley

Hi, Lizzy. Heard u r coming over today! Yay!

Lizzy

Hi! I am!

Send

Bingley

It's been forever—8 months! I haven't 👀 u since the Netherfield ball on <u>November 26!</u>

Lizzy

Wow, u r right. And so specific. 😏

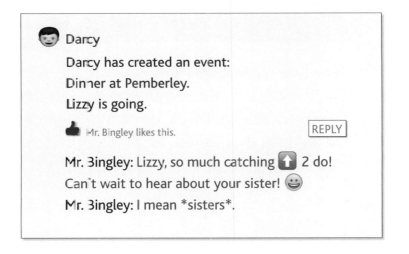

🙂 Darcy

Darcy has created an event:

Dinner at Pemberley.

Lizzy is going.

👍 Mr. Bingley likes this.   REPLY

Mr. Bingley: Lizzy, so much catching ⬆️ 2 do! Can't wait to hear about your sister! 😀

Mr. Bingley: I mean *sisters*.

Mrs. Gardiner

Notice anything funny?

Mr. Gardiner

Darcy?

Send

Mrs. Gardiner

Yes. He's obvi in 😍 w/ Lizzy. 💘

Mr. Gardiner

100%

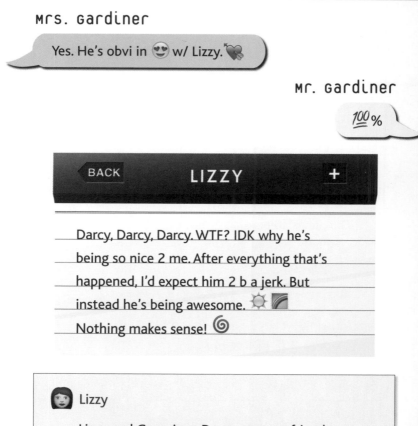

BACK **LIZZY** +

Darcy, Darcy, Darcy. WTF? IDK why he's being so nice 2 me. After everything that's happened, I'd expect him 2 b a jerk. But instead he's being awesome. ☀️🌄 Nothing makes sense! 🌀

🧑 Lizzy

Lizzy and Georgiana Darcy are now friends.

👍 Darcy likes this.   REPLY

Send

miss Bingley

Man, Lizzy looked terrible today, huh, Darcy? Almost didn't recognize her! 😂

Darcy

I didn't notice anything different.

miss Bingley

Srsly she's nothing 2 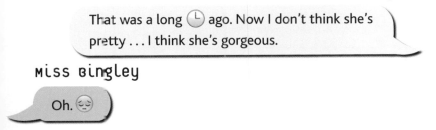 abt. Her features r boring: 👀 👃 👄. Remember when u said Lizzy was pretty? LOLZ. You may as well say her mother is smart! #Bwahaha #EvilLaughter

Darcy

That was a long 🕐 ago. Now I don't think she's pretty . . . I think she's gorgeous.

miss Bingley

Oh. 😔

Send

From: Jane Bennet
To: Lizzy Bennet
Subject: We're Ruined

Lydia and Wickham have run away together. 💒!!!
Mom is FREAKING out. This will RUIN us. We'll
be old maids 4ever if Wickham doesn't 👰 her.
We don't have 💰, so maybe he's doing it 4
#TheRightReasons? Please come 🏠 asap!! And
bring our aunt & uncle! Dad needs help trying to
find Lydia in London. 💩 We're so 🍄ed.

Darcy

> Thanks 4 coming over last night, Lizzy.

Lizzy

> Can't talk. I need 2 find my aunt & uncle asap!

Darcy

> Are you all right? Do you want a glass of 🍷?

Lizzy

> No, no. I'm not 😒. I just got terrible 📰. 😭

Send

Darcy

???

Lizzy

My sister's 🏃 off w/ Wickham. U can figure out the rest. 🎁 I can't believe I didn't tell any1 what a 💩 person he is. 😈

Darcy

OMG NO. Can I help??

Lizzy

No. My dad & uncle will go look 4 her.

Darcy

I'm so, so sorry. 😔

Lizzy

Me 2. Please don't say anything 2 anyone. 🙏

Darcy

I promise I won't. 🙊

Send

My 👨‍👩‍👧‍👦 is a disgrace. 🙄 Darcy can never 💔 me now. 😭 Things were just starting 2 go my way & now THIS. Sux that in losing him I realize how I rly feel. 👰💔 #SingleBecause

---

👩 **Mrs. Bennet**

If we had all gone 2 Brighton for the summer, none of this would have ever happened! I'm so upset I can't leave my room! 😖

👍 Lady Catherine de Bourgh likes this.   REPLY

Lizzy: Mom, this is all Lydia's fault!
Jane: We'll probably see her change her relationship status asap. #Refresh
Collins: I don't mean to be rude . . . but it'd probably b better if she had died, huh? So glad I didn't u, Lizzy lol. (No offense.)

Send

Mary Bennet

REPLY

Lizzy

Daddy, I m so sorry this happened.

Mr. Bennet

Don't be. have no one to blame but myself. You were right about everything. Go ahead and say you told me so.

Lizzy

I would never. 😔

Send

! >>> Message forwarded from Mr. Bennet to Lizzy

From: Mr. Gardiner
To: Mr. Bennet
Subject: Good News (& Bad News)

I found Lydia and Wickham! I convinced them that they had to marry, now that they've been living in sin together. 💏 But there is 1 condition: you have to promise Lydia an inheritance when you die. 😵 They're not asking for much. Seems that Wickham's not as broke as we thought he was. If you agree, Lydia will get married today. 👰 😦

Lizzy

OMG! What are u going 2 📝 back?

Mr. Bennet

I can't believe Wickham asked for so little. I need to know (1) how much money Gardiner put down, and (2) how I am ever going to repay him. 😔

Send

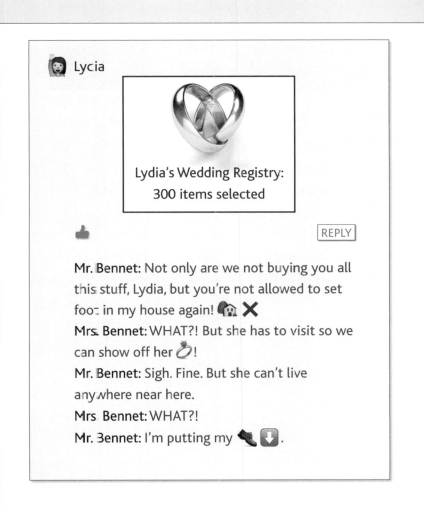

Lycia

Lydia's Wedding Registry:
300 items selected

👍   REPLY

Mr. Bennet: Not only are we not buying you all this stuff, Lydia, but you're not allowed to set foot in my house again! 🏠❌

Mrs. Bennet: WHAT?! But she has to visit so we can show off her 💍!

Mr. Bennet: Sigh. Fine. But she can't live anywhere near here.

Mrs Bennet: WHAT?!

Mr. Bennet: I'm putting my 👞⬇️.

Send

Can't stop thinking about Darcy. He and I could have been the happiest couple in the 🌍 if it wasn't 4 this bull💩 w/ Lydia. I wish he didn't know the truth! 😭 I should have kept my mouth shut. 😶

✅ Lydia and Wickham have checked into Longbourn.
👍 Mrs. Bennet likes this.

🙋 Lydia

Lydia has changed her relationship status from Single to Married. #SorrySisters

👍 REPLY

Mrs. Bennet: OMG!!!!!!!!!!!!!!!! YOU'RE MARRIED!!!!!!!!!!! 🍀 Hooray! 👰 💍 💐
Lizzy: Srsly, Mom? SMH.
Jane: Wickham must rly 🖤 Lydia . . . right? 😞

Send

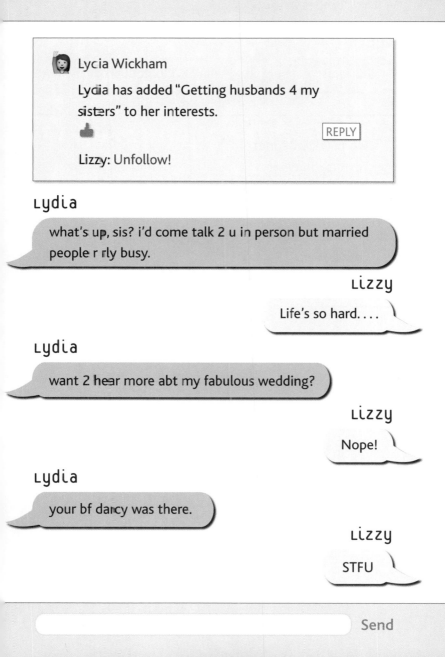

Lycia Wickham

Lydia has added "Getting husbands 4 my sisters" to her interests.

👍   REPLY

Lizzy: Unfollow!

Lydia

what's up, sis? i'd come talk 2 u in person but married people r rly busy.

Lizzy

Life's so hard. . . .

Lydia

want 2 hear more abt my fabulous wedding?

Lizzy

Nope!

Lydia

your bf darcy was there.

Lizzy

STFU

Send

Lydia

💩 i wasn't supposed to tell you. i forgot i promised not 2.

From: Lizzy Bennet
To: Mrs. Gardiner
Subject: Darcy Cameo

Hi, Auntie.
Is it true that Darcy was @ Lydia's wedding? I need
details! Thx!
Your favorite niece xx

Send

From: Mrs. Gardiner
To: Lizzy Bennet
Subject: Re: Darcy Cameo

Yes, Lizzy. Darcy found Wickham & Lydia and tried to talk them out of their 🌀 plans. He tried to make Lydia leave, but she wouldn't. So he made sure they got married 👰. Darcy paid off Wickham's debts 💲 and got a new job for him. Your uncle wanted to pay off the debt 💸, but Darcy insisted. He felt his pride was responsible for everything.

Mrs. Gardiner

PS: Don't be mad I didn't tell you sooner. I wasn't supposed to say anything. But now that you know, isn't Darcy the greatest? If I were young and single . . . 😌

Send

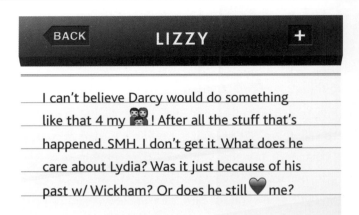

BACK LIZZY +

I can't believe Darcy would do something like that 4 my 👨‍👩‍👧‍👦! After all the stuff that's happened. SMH. I don't get it. What does he care about Lydia? Was it just because of his past w/ Wickham? Or does he still 🖤 me?

✅ Bingley has checked into Netherfield.

Lizzy

Jane! Did you see that Bingley's back in town?

Jane

Yes, I wish Mom would stop reminding me. Just when things were starting to get easier, he comes back and all the old feelings resurface. 💔

Send

✅ Bingley and Darcy have checked into Longbourn.

Mrs. Bennet: So glad ur here, Bingley! Make yourself @ 🏡!!

Jane: Don't 4get about Darcy, Mom!

Mrs. Bennet: Darcy, too, I guess.

Lizzy: Mom, please.

Bingley: Jane, I can't wait 2 👀 u! From ur pics, u are looking like an 😇 as always.

Jane: Bingley, u sure know how 2 make a girl 😳.

Mrs. Bennet: We r all SO happy 2 have you back in town, Bingley. We thought you were never coming back!! So much has happened!!! Did you see Charlotte and Lydia got married???

Darcy: Didn't know they were each other's type, lol.

Lizzy: Ha!

Mrs. Bennet: Huh?

Lizzy: Bingley, how long do you plan to stay in town?

Bingley: A few weeks, I think.

Mrs. Bennet: Ur welcome 2 come here anytime u'd like! 😉 Come over 4 dinner 1 night this week.

Bingley: Will do! 👍

Send

BACK **LIZZY** +

Darcy didn't say 1 word 2 me when he was here. 😢 I wanted 2 thank him 4 what he did 4 my 👪, but couldn't find the right 🕐. It's so hard 2 get a read on him. 👓 📖

Jane

The worst is behind us, Lizzy. We survived 👀 Darcy & Bingley w/o falling 2 pieces! And now every1 will say we r just friends. 🤍

Lizzy

#FamousLastWords Do u rly expect me 2 believe that? Bingley's obvi more in 😍 w/ u than before!

Jane

You think??

Lizzy

I know. 😉

Send

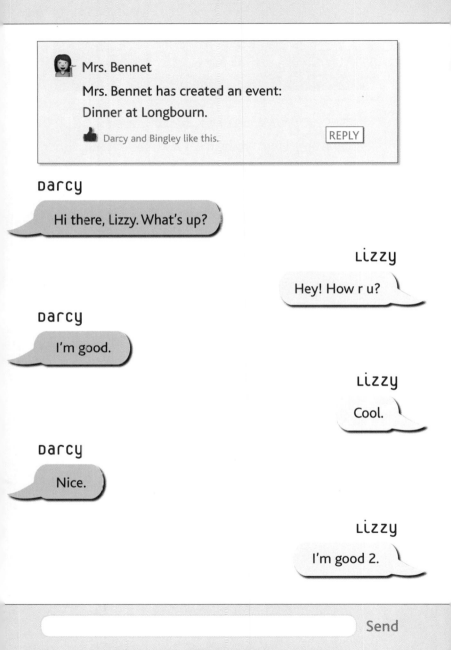

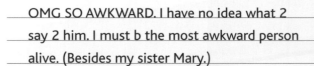

OMG SO AWKWARD. I have no idea what 2 say 2 him. I must b the most awkward person alive. (Besides my sister Mary.)

 Mrs. Bennet
Dinner was perfect!!! Even Darcy admitted it!!! And everyone agreed that Jane looked stunning! #GreatSuccess

👍 | REPLY |

☑ Mr. Bingley has checked into Longbourn.

👍 Jane and Mrs. Bennet like this.

Mr. Bingley: Jane, can we talk later?
Jane: Of course!
Mrs. Bennet: OMG! Bingley, are u going 2 2 Jane? OMG, u totally r, I know it!

Send

Lizzy

😃 #BestDayEver

Jane

🖤🖤🖤 Ahhhh!! I couldn't b happier! #Blessed

And do u know what else? He told me he had no clue I was in London last yr!

Lizzy

Rly?!

Send

jane

Must have been his sisters trying 2 tear us apart. 💔 But no matter, I will have the last laugh. 😂

Lizzy

That's probably the meanest thing you've ever said. Bwahaha! LOVE IT.

jane

🙈

He told me he was in love with me all last year. He thought I didn't love him back! Can you believe it??

Lizzy

No, I can't. . . . But I'm so happy it all worked out! #OTP

Lady catherine de Bourgh

Elizabeth Bennet. —LCdB

Lizzy

Yes, this is Lizzy.

Send

Lady Catherine de Bourgh

Your sister just got engaged, and now I hear you are about to get engaged to my nephew Darcy. Impossible! Did he or did he not propose? —LCdB

Lizzy

U just said it was impossible.

Lady Catherine de Bourgh

DO YOU KNOW WHO I AM? I have a right to know what Darcy is doing. —LCdB

Lizzy

Yeah, I know who you are. You sign all your texts. But u don't have a right 2 know what I'm doing.

Lady Catherine de Bourgh

Mark my words. Darcy is getting married to MY daughter. —LCdB

Lizzy

So why r u txting me?

Send

Lady catherine de Bourgh

We've been planning this since they were babies. Literally!!! I'm not going to let this fall apart because of someone of inferior birth! —LCdB

Lizzy

Not my problem. If he wants to 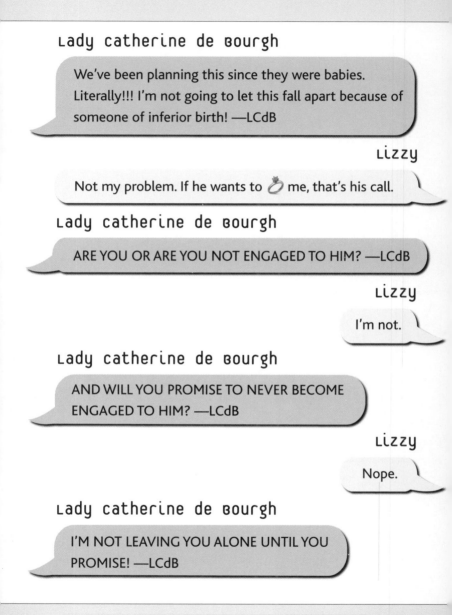 me, that's his call.

Lady catherine de Bourgh

ARE YOU OR ARE YOU NOT ENGAGED TO HIM? —LCdB

Lizzy

I'm not.

Lady catherine de Bourgh

AND WILL YOU PROMISE TO NEVER BECOME ENGAGED TO HIM? —LCdB

Lizzy

Nope.

Lady catherine de Bourgh

I'M NOT LEAVING YOU ALONE UNTIL YOU PROMISE! —LCdB

Send

Lizzy

Well, I'm not going 2 promise, so u'd better have a good plan.

Lady catherine de Bourgh

YOU WANT TO DO THIS THE HARD WAY? I WILL TELL EVERYONE ABOUT LYDIA'S ELOPEMENT. —LCdB

Lizzy

That's it! U have ✖ed the line.

Lady catherine de Bourgh

WILL YOU PROMISE NOT TO MARRY HIM?? —LCdB

Lizzy

I will do whatever makes *me* happy.

#ByeFelicia

Lady catherine de Bourgh

WE'RE NOT DONE HERE. —LCcB

🚫 Lizzy has added Lady Catherine de Bourgh to Blocked Callers List.

Send

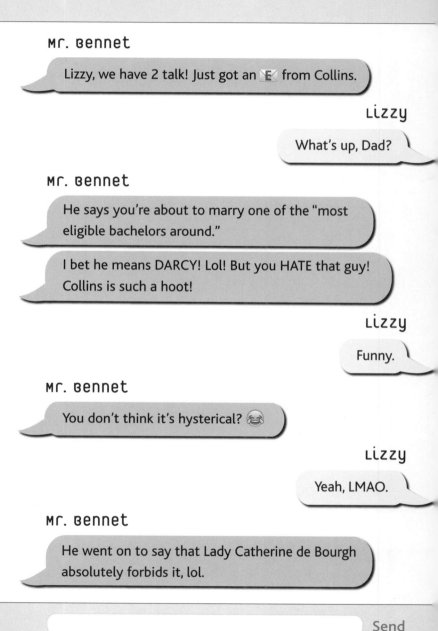

Lizzy

Lol.

Mr. Bennet

He also told me that we should disown Lydia, as is our "Christian duty."

Lizzy

Okay, that one is actually funny! 😜

✅ Darcy and Bingley have checked into Longbourn.

👍 Lizzy and Jane like this.

Lizzy

Darcy!

Darcy

Hey.

Lizzy

I don't know how 2 thank u 4 all u have done 2 save Lydia's rep.

Send

Darcy

😞 I didn't want u 2 know.

Lizzy

Lydia has a big 👄. TY so, so much. My 👪 owes u 1.

Darcy

NBD. Truth is I only did it 4 u, Lizzy.

Lizzy

!!!

Darcy

Look, I gotta know. Do u still hate me? 😠 If so, that's fine & I'll never ask again. But I'm still in 🖤 w/ u.

Lizzy

I don't hate u at all, Darcy.

Darcy

Rly?

Lizzy

I'm in 🖤 w/ u! 👩‍❤️‍👨

Send

Darcy

😄 😄 😄 Even after everything that happened w/ my crazy aunt? I 👂 she threatened u. SMH.

Lizzy

Haha, yeah.

Darcy

She's crazy, but her visit gave me hope! 🌈 If you didn't 💚 me, then u would've just told her so. 😉

Lizzy

Well, I had no trouble cutting u down to ur face, so y not in front of ur whole 👪? Haha

Darcy

I deserved everything u said. When u told me I acted like a jerk, and that there was nothing I could say 2 make u accept my 💍 . . . BURN. I read back those msgs a lot.

Lizzy

OMG delete them immediately.

Darcy

Was it my 💌 that changed ur mind?

Send

Lizzy

It changed everything.

Darcy

Sry if it hurt ur feelings. Delete it, please!

Lizzy

I will if you want me to. 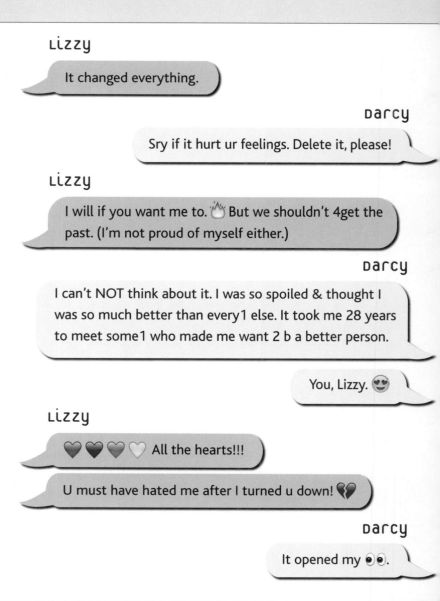 But we shouldn't 4get the past. (I'm not proud of myself either.)

Darcy

I can't NOT think about it. I was so spoiled & thought I was so much better than every1 else. It took me 28 years to meet some1 who made me want 2 b a better person.

You, Lizzy. 😍

Lizzy

🩶🖤💚🤍 All the hearts!!!

U must have hated me after I turned u down! 💔

Darcy

It opened my 👀.

Send

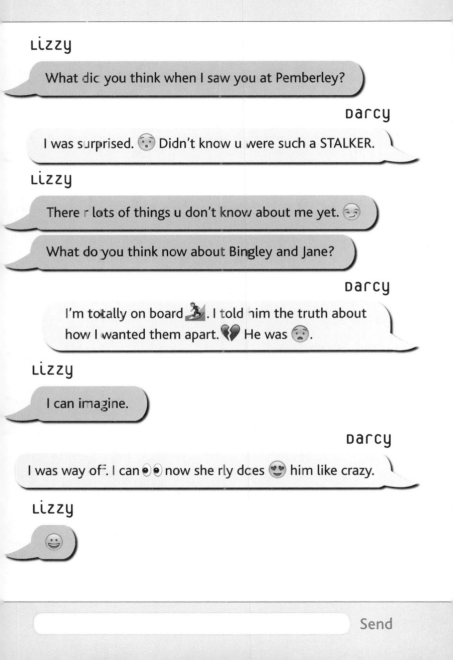

Lizzy

What did you think when I saw you at Pemberley?

Darcy

I was surprised. 😯 Didn't know u were such a STALKER.

Lizzy

There r lots of things u don't know about me yet. 😏

What do you think now about Bingley and Jane?

Darcy

I'm totally on board 🏄. I told him the truth about how I wanted them apart. 💔 He was 😧.

Lizzy

I can imagine.

Darcy

I was way off. I can 👀 now she rly does 😍 him like crazy.

Lizzy

😀

Send

Darcy

He was 😠 when I told him she was in London the whole 🕐 and we didn't tell him. But now he's forgiven me. #Whew

Lizzy

I'm so happy 2 hear it. I'm so happy w/ *everything*!

Darcy

Me 2. 🖤

● ● ●

Jane

Where r u?

Lizzy

Darcy and I went for a walk. I have ....

We're engaged!

Send

Jane

WHAT?!?! 🙀 Are u sure this is what u want?

Lizzy

Yes, we're going 2 b so happy 4ever! 👨‍❤️‍👨 We're madly in 💘.

Jane

U have 2 tell me everything! When did u change ur mind?

Lizzy

I mean, have u seen Pemberley? 💰💰💰

Jane

Haha

Lizzy

Jk, but yes, I am head over 👠👠. He's my person. Wait until I tell u the whole 📖.

Jane

Meet me downstairs asap!

● ● ●

Send

Mr. Bennet

Hey, Lizzy, Darcy came by. What the ☁️😈☁️?? You're ENGAGED?

Lizzy

Yes. We're in 💚. Will u give us ur blessing?

Mr. Bennet

Of course, if you're *100*% sure.

Lizzy

I am, Dad. 😄 It's a really long story, but trust me—it's the right decision!

BTW, Darcy was the 1 who paid Wickham's debts in London and set things right with Lydia.

Mr. Bennet

Darcy?! I really thought it was ur uncle. In that 💼, I'm 😄 2 have Darcy as a future son-in-law.

Lizzy

👍

Send

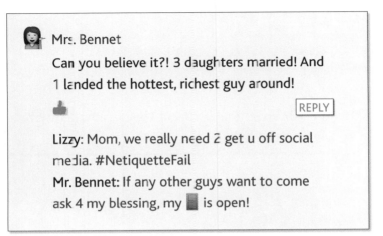

Mrs. Bennet
Can you believe it?! 3 daughters married! And 1 landed the hottest, richest guy around!

👍   REPLY

Lizzy: Mom, we really need 2 get u off social media. #NetiquetteFail
Mr. Bennet: If any other guys want to come ask 4 my blessing, my 🚪 is open!

Lizzy
Darcy, tell me how u fell 4 me.

Darcy
I can't 📍 the exact moment. But I was in the middle b4 I knew I'd begun. 👫

Lizzy
Tell me the truth. Did you like that I was mean 2 u? 😏

Darcy
I liked that u could hold ur own. 😏

Send

Lizzy

R u going 2 tell ur aunt about us? —LB

Darcy

Haha, I've been putting it off, but I just need 2 get it over w/ and send the .

Lizzy

Do u want me 2 sit next 2 u and admire ur most excellent writing? 😉

Darcy

Ha! 😘

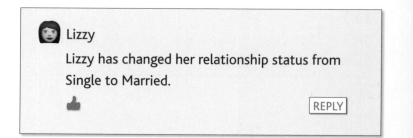

👍   REPLY

Send

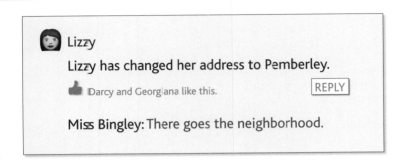

Lizzy

Lizzy has changed her address to Pemberley.

👍 Darcy and Georgiana like this. | REPLY |

Miss Bingley: There goes the neighborhood.

🏠 Netherfield Estate is now for sale.

Lizzy: Jane! So happy u & ur hubby r moving closer
to us! 🚚 🏠 😃

From: Lydia Wickham (Bennet)
To: Lizzy Darcy (Bennet)
Subject: money, please

hooray! ur FINALLY married! and rich 2! let me know
if u have 💸 2 spare, bc Wickham and I could use it.
not 2 much. no worries if not.

ttyl,
lydia xo

Send

From: Lizzy Darcy (Bennet)
To: Lydia Wickham (Bennet)
Re: money, please

Um, no. 👋🏻

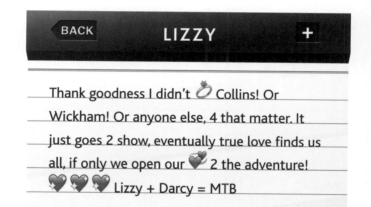

BACK   LIZZY   +

Thank goodness I didn't 💍 Collins! Or
Wickham! Or anyone else, 4 that matter. It
just goes 2 show, eventually true love finds us
all, if only we open our 💕 2 the adventure!
🖤🖤🖤 Lizzy + Darcy = MTB

Send

The 411 for Those
Not in the Know

411: Information

ASAP: As Soon As Possible

BFF: Best Friend Forever

BRB: Be Right Back

BTW: By The Way

FML: F*ck My Life

FOMO: Fear Of Missing Out

FTW: For The Win

FYI: For Your Information

G2G: Got To Go

GTFO: Get The F*ck Out

ICYMI: In Case You Missed It

IDK: I Don't Know

IMHO: In My Humble Opinion

IRL: In Real Life

JK: Just Kidding

LMAO: Laughing My A$$ Off

Send

LOL: Laughing Out Loud

LOLZ: Laughing Out Loud (ironically)

MTB: Meant To Be

NBD: No Big Deal

NTM: Not Much

NVMD: Nevermind

OMG: Oh My God

OTP: One True Pairing

OTW: On The Way

SMH: Shaking My Head

STFU: Shut The F*ck Up

TBH: To Be Honest

TL;DR: Too Long; Didn't Read

TTYL: Talk To You Later

TY: Thank You

WTF: What The F*ck?

YOLO: You Only Live Once

Send

some emotions you might find in this book

😠 Angry

😣 Anguish

😅 Anxious

😖 Confounded

😎 Cool

😂 Crying Laughing

😵 Dead (or Dying)

😞 Disappointed

😳 Embarrassed

😈 Evil (Devil)

😘 Flirty

😉 Friendly (wink, wink)

😜 Goofy

😃 Happy

😍 In Love (and/or Lovestruck)

Send

😇 Innocent

😰 Nervous

😡 Really Angry

😔 Sad

😢 Sad (and Crying)

😭 Sad (and Sobbing)

😱 Scared (and Screaming)

😬 Sheepish (and/or Grimacing)

😧 Shocked

😷 Sick

😶 Silent

😴 Sleepy

😏 Sly

😯 Surprised

😒 Unamused

😟 Worried

Send

COURTNEY CARBONE studied English and creative writing in the US and Australia before becoming a children's book writer and editor in New York City. Her favorite things include Brit lit, trivia nights, board games, stand-up comedy, improv, bookstores, libraries, brick-oven pizza, salted-caramel macarons, theme parties, sharks, puns, portmanteaus, and '90s pop culture. 😎

🐦 @CBCarbone
CourtneyCarbone.com

JANE AUSTEN was born in England in 1775. Her best-known works are *Pride and Prejudice*, *Sense and Sensibility*, and *Emma*. Filled with wit and social commentary, Austen's novels are not only critically acclaimed but also extremely popular. Her books are some of the most widely read and beloved in the English language. 🖤 📚

Send